by Terry Collins   illustrated by Barry Goldberg

based on the original teleplay "Birth of a Salesman"

by Steven Banks

Simon Spotlight/Nickelodeon

New York   London   Toronto   Sydney   Singapore

Based on the TV series *The Adventures of Jimmy Neutron, Boy Genius*® as seen on Nickelodeon®

 SIMON SPOTLIGHT
An imprint of Simon & Schuster Children's Publishing Division
1230 Avenue of the Americas, New York, NY 10020
Copyright © 2003 Viacom International Inc. All rights reserved. NICKELODEON,
The Adventures of Jimmy Neutron, Boy Genius, and all related titles, logos, and
characters are trademarks of Viacom International Inc. All rights reserved including
the right of reproduction in whole or in part in any form.
SIMON SPOTLIGHT and colophon are registered trademarks of Simon & Schuster.
Manufactured in the United States of America
First Edition 10 9 8 7 6 5 4 3 2 1
ISBN 0-689-85300-9

Jimmy Neutron cleared his throat and stood tall in the Retroville Elementary schoolyard.

"Ladies and gentlemen, kids of all ages, prepare to feast your eyes on the greatest thing ever beheld!" he announced, kneeling down to open his backpack.

Jimmy held out a handful of gum.

"What—an invention of yours that actually works?" Cindy said with a laugh.

"Noooo! Er, I mean, yes," Jimmy said. "I present to you the latest and greatest Neutron invention . . . Book Bubblegum!"

"Oh, brother," Libby said.

"Here, try some. I modified my shrink ray with a digital blender and a pocket spell-checker to reduce the contents of different books to gum form," Jimmy explained.

"So?" Cindy asked.

"So, chew a piece, and read a great book at the same time!"

Sheen took a piece, popped it into his mouth, and began to chew.

"Tastes kinda . . . fishy," Sheen said as the salty flavor flooded his brain. "Call me Ishmael! It's the great white whale! I'll get ye, Moby Dick!"

"Mine tastes like fried chicken," Cindy cried. "Oh, Ashley! Oh, Rhett! Tomorrow is another day! I don't know nuthin' 'bout birthin' babies!"

"Mmm . . . mine's all mushy," Carl sighed, his eyes dreamy. "But, soft! What light through yonder window breaks? It is the east, and Juliet is the sun!"

"Ewwwww," Libby said, crossing her arms. "No way am I playing Juliet to Carl's Romeo! Come on, Cindy, school is about to start!"

"Let me remind you, class, that tomorrow is the annual Fifth-Grade Bookworm Contest," Miss Fowl said. "And I'm happy to announce we have two wonderful prizes for the winners."

"What do I get for winning first place?" Jimmy asked.

"Don't polish that trophy yet, Neutron," Cindy said.

Miss Fowl continued, "The student who answers the most questions correctly wins a free all-access pass to the Retroland amusement park."

"Been there, done that," Jimmy said, trying not to yawn.

"And, for the first time ever, you will be allowed one spit from The Eye-in-the-Sky ride onto the guest of your choice below *without* doing hard time."

Every kid in the room gaped in disbelief.

"Second place wins a handcrafted, one-of-a-kind, goldazium-plated Ultra Lord action figure, donated by Blast-Off Toys and Novelties."

"Gulp!" Sheen swallowed. "Oh, my god, oh, my god!" Sheen said in awe. "That—that's the *rarest* Ultra Lord figure of them all!"

On the way home from school, Jimmy caught up with Cindy.

"That contest is a Neutron lock," Jimmy said. "I'm already saving up extra spit for my ride in the sky!"

Cindy snorted. "As if, boy blunder! No way am I missing the chance to lob a wet one onto your pointed noggin!"

"An impressive display of delusional thinking, but everyone knows I'm winning this contest."

"Oh, really?" Cindy sneered. "Then let the games begin!"

Later that day Sheen thought about the possibility of taking home the Ultra Lord toy from the contest. "No way can I win, but why couldn't I take second place?" he muttered. "I gotta have that Ultra Lord action figure! It—it's still in mint condition in the box!"

From the living room Sheen's grandmother called out, "Sheeeeen! Your little show about the man in the funny costume is on!"

Sheen ran into the living room. "Grandma, that *funny costume* belongs to only the greatest action hero ever!" Sheen said.

"Poppycock! In my day, kids read books for fun!" Sheen's grandmother retorted. "Plus books are educational!"

Sheen turned from the television. "Grandma, that's it!" he cried. "You've told me how I can win the Ultra Lord figure of my dreams!"

That night Sheen raced over to Jimmy's secret laboratory.

"Jimmy! Jimmy! You gotta help me!" Sheen called.

"Not now, Sheen," Jimmy said. "I need to brush up on my Greek mythology for tomorrow's contest. Besides, isn't *Ultra Lord: The Animated Series* on right now?"

BOOK
BUBBLEGUM

"Yes, but that's not important," Sheen said. "I can watch *Ultra Lord* later!" Jimmy blinked his eyes in surprise. Sheen never missed an episode of *Ultra Lord*. "What's the scoop?" he asked.

"I've got to place second in that contest tomorrow," Sheen said. "I figure, if I chew enough book gum, I'll be smart enough to win that goldazium Ultra Lord action figure."

"Yes, well, this would be a fascinating experiment in the use of compressed education," Jimmy said.

Two hours later Sheen was still chewing his first piece of book gum.

"Behold, brave knight. Yon liege's jaws are starting to get tired from chewing," Sheen said, sighing.

"You have to chew until all the flavor is gone to make sure you've read the entire book!" Jimmy said. "Come on, you've got a whole library to go!"

Sheen groaned. At this rate, he'd be chewing all night—unless he could speed up the process!

"Gimme that gum, Goddard," he ordered.

"Bark!" Goddard said, chasing after Sheen.

Sheen tilted his head back.

"Pukin' Pluto, Sheen! What are you doing?" Jimmy asked.

"I'm taking a crash course for Ultra Lord fans across the galaxy!" Sheen replied, pouring all of the book gum into his mouth.

"Stop!" Jimmy cried, horrified. "It's too dangerous! The human brain can't handle that much information at once!"

Sheen's eyes bulged as he chewed the enormous wad of gum. *CHOMP!* The story of Cinderella squirted into his mind! *CHOMP!* The Little Engine That Could climbed the hill of his brain!

As Sheen chewed and chewed, books collided in his overworked brain cells.

"Once upon a time! It was the best of times, it was the worst of times! The porridge is just right!" Sheen babbled.

Jimmy gasped. "Experiment meltdown! He's suffering a literature overload! It's a good thing the effects of the book gum wear off in twenty-four hours."

"Tom Sawyer, you stay away from that
Huck Finn! Elementary, my dear Watson!"
Sheen paused, then fell over in a heap.
Jimmy helped his friend to his feet.
"Let's get you home, bookworm," Jimmy said.
"Good night, moon!" Sheen groaned.

The next day Jimmy went to visit Sheen.

"How's the wonderful world of reading?"

"My jaw hurts," Sheen replied. "I'm just glad Grandma didn't make me go to school today."

"You didn't miss much," Jimmy said. "Just that dumb ol' contest."

"My Ultra Lord figure!" Sheen said. "My head was stuffed so full of knowledge, I forgot all about him!"

"I still say the questions were rigged," Jimmy said. "I demanded a recount!"

"Why? I thought you couldn't lose!" Sheen said, and then he grinned. "Don't tell me Cindy Vortex beat—"

"She didn't beat me!" Jimmy protested. "Seems that I must have skipped *Little Women* on my reading list."

"By the way, I got you a present," Jimmy said, pulling a box out of his knapsack.

Sheen cradled the goldazium-plated Ultra Lord action figure.

"So, do you like it?" Jimmy asked.

"I think you're the best pal a guy could have, Jimmy," Sheen replied.

"You know it," Jimmy said. "Hey, want a piece of gum?"

"No, thanks," Sheen said. "Gum's bad for your teeth . . . and your brain!"